Esther Brown Tiffany

An Autograph Letter

A comedy in three acts

Esther Brown Tiffany

An Autograph Letter
A comedy in three acts

ISBN/EAN: 9783744781640

Printed in Europe, USA, Canada, Australia, Japan

Cover: Foto ©Andreas Hilbeck / pixelio.de

More available books at **www.hansebooks.com**

AN

AUTOGRAPH LETTER

A Comedy in Three Acts

BY

ESTHER B. TIFFANY,

AUTHOR OF "ANITA'S TRIAL," "A RICE PUDDING," "THE WAY
TO HIS POCKET," "YOUNG MR. PRITCHARD,"
"THAT PATRICK," ETC.

BOSTON

Walter H. Baker & Co.

1889.

CHARACTERS.

JOHN MASTERS.

HAL MASTERS, *nephew to John Masters.*

PHILIP STAUNTON.

DR. PROCTER.

SHERIFF.

PRISCILLA MAY.

HELEN STAUNTON, *daughter to Staunton.*

LIBBY MASTERS, *sister to John Masters.*

MRS. GRIGGS.

MAID.

AN AUTOGRAPH LETTER.

ACT I.

SCENE. — STAUNTON'S *room in a lodging-house, meagrely furnished. Door*, L., *in flat; door*, R.; *window*, R., *in flat; table*, R.; *easy-chair*, L.; *secretary, to lock, at back.* HELEN *and* DR. PROCTER *discovered.*

DR. PROCTER (C., *pompously*). As I before elucidated to you, my dear young lady, skilled competence and proficiency — in other words, a trained nurse.

HELEN (*down* R. *at table*). But I love nursing.

DR. PROCT. You are — permit the personality — excessively youthful, absolutely inexperienced.

HEL. Why, I'm almost eighteen.

DR. PROCT. And your father's condition necessitates unceasing supervision. These — er — drops at intervals of — um — half an hour.

HEL. Yes, sir.

DR. PROCT. And two-thirds of a wine-glass of old port every two hours.

HEL. Yes, sir.

DR. PROCT. Exercise great discretion concerning the port. Gross & Paige keep the only port in the city in the least suitable for a refined and delicate palate. Then, any trifle that might tempt the capricious appetite of a convalescent. Er — um — Hamburg grapes — er — peaches — the breast of a partridge — er — er — dairy cream — in short, any little trifle of that character.

HEL. Yes, sir. (*Aside.*) And only ten dollars in the house!

DR. PROCT. Following which treatment, a trip to the South as soon as locomotion appears desirable. Above all,

3

no undue excitement. In other words, no cerebral per-
turbation. You — eh — comprehend? I make myself — eh
— lucid?

HEL. Yes, sir. I think I understand. (*Aside.*) Though,
where the money is to come from I do not understand.

DR. PROCT. You may expect me in the morning. Er —
good-day — Miss — er — er — Staunton.

HEL. Good-morning, Dr. Procter. (*Exit* DR. PROCTER
D. L. *in* F.) Wine! Hamburg grapes! A journey to the
South! Poor father! And our purse growing lighter every
hour. How much have I? (*Counts her money.*) Ten dollars and forty cents — and after that is gone! Ten dollars
all that is left from the sale of that valuable autograph letter
of Washington's! It brought us one hundred dollars, but
how quickly one hundred dollars go! Could I borrow from
Hal? (*Goes* L.) No, no ; from him least of all He must
not even suspect our strait. He sees me well dressed — he
does not fancy that these are the last of all my pretty clothes.
Father always would give me such lovely things. even when
he couldn't afford it. (*A knock at* D. *in* F.) Come in.

(*Enter* MRS. GRIGGS. D. *in* F.)

MRS G. (*at door*). The young feller that's keepin' company with you 's ringin' at the front-door bell.

HEL. Mrs. Griggs, if you please, there is no young man
keeping company with me.

MRS. G. Oh, they ain't! Well, then, if they ain't — if he
ain't — and he's quite easy in his pocket, I should say — I'll
just trouble you for that rent ; that's all.

HEL. Mrs. Griggs, I must ask you to wait a little longer.

MRS. G. Wait? And haven't I been waitin', patient as
a lamb, bein' convinced that young feller meant business,
and would hand over so'thin' handsome soon as you was
engaged?

HEL. Mrs. Griggs, if ever — (HAL *appears at* D. *in* F.)

HAL. Good-morning, Miss Helen. Oh, Mrs. Griggs,
good-morning.

HEL. Good-morning, Mr. Masters.

MRS. G. We was just talkin' about you.

HAL. That's what made my ear burn so.

HEL. Come in, Mr. Masters. (*Goes up.*)

MRS. G. I'd like to have a few words with you in private,
Mr. Masters, when you're through here.

HAL. Oh, certainly, Mrs. Griggs.

HEL. (*drawing him in and shutting the door on* MRS. G.). Promise me you won't let her speak to you.

HAL. I can't say I'm very anxious for an interview, but why —

HEL. Because I — well, because —

HAL. That's quite sufficient reason. I'll avoid Mrs. Griggs. I'll sneak out and in the back way. I'll — but I beg your pardon, how's your father ? (*Comes down to* C.)

HEL. About the same. (*Down to* R.)

HAL. In bed still ?

HEL. No, up and around, but feverish and restless. Something seems preying on his mind. He wakes and calls out at night in such an agonized way —

HAL. Can I see him ?

HEL. No, he's asleep now.

HAL. Isn't there anything I can do ? What has Old Port ordered for him ?

HEL. Old Port ?

HAL. I beg his pardon, Dr. Procter. Old Port is what we call him at the Medical School, because he cures everything, from a sprained finger to lockjaw, with a glass of old port. I'm sure, now, he's ordered your father some old port.

HEL. Yes, he has.

HAL. I thought so. Now, I've got in the cellar at home — that is, we've got — my Uncle John, you know ; I say we because he goes shares with everything —-

HEL. What a dear old gentleman your uncle must be.

HAL. Old gentleman ! Why, Uncle John is barely forty, and hasn't a gray hair.

HEL. Except what you have caused him.

HAL. Oh, that kind doesn't count ! But this old port of his — I'll bring you round a half a dozen bottles.

HEL. Oh, no.

HAL. Oh, yes. Good-by. I'll run round now. (*Goes up to door and comes back.*) Oh, by the way —

HEL. Yes.

HAL. There are some things we don't go shares in — Uncle John and I.

HEL. Debts ?

HAL. Debts ? No, bless him, if I had any, he'd insist on taking them all himself. No — secrets !

HEL. So he has a cellar full of secrets as well as of port ?

HAL. Uncle John, secrets? What an idea! You ought to see him! He's a complete book-worm, except when he's off fishing and tramping; and then he's the jolliest, drollest —but secrets, the kind of secrets I mean—why, do you know, he can't endure women.

HEL. Why. I thought you said he was nice!

HAL. But, then, perhaps Aunt Libby—that's his only sister—has something to do with his opinion of women. (*Goes up to door and returns.*) You—you haven't asked me what my secret is.

HEL. It wouldn't be a secret if you told me, would it?

HAL. There's nothing cosier than a secret just for two; is there, now? (*Takes her hand.*)

HEL. It depends on the two. (*Draws away.*)

HAL. Yes, of course; and then, when one of the two is dependent on (*aside*) Uncle John, who holds the purse-strings. (*Aloud.*) But I must go. I'll be right back with the port. I'll bring it round in six trips, a bottle at a time. Good-by.

HEL. Good-by.

HAL. Good-by. (*Aside.*) I'll have to bottle myself up, or— (*Exit D. L. in F.*)

HEL. That dreadful Mrs. Griggs. (*Up C.*) If she should speak to him! (*Looking out of door.*) There she is now; he sees her—he's running. He pretends not to notice her. She's calling after him. He won t hear. There, he's out of sight. (*Down R.*)

(MRS. G. *appears at door.*)

MRS. G. Rather hard of hearin', that young feller, ain't he?

HEL. Oh, Mrs. Griggs, I must just step out for a moment to the druggist. Father is asleep, but if he should wake and call, will you come in?

MRS. G. Yes, I'll be round. (*Exit.*)

HEL. (*looking in at chamber door, R.*). Yes, he's fast asleep still. I'll only be gone a moment. I would have asked Mr. Masters to get the medicine for me, but that nice old druggist is so kind, and calls me "my child," and gives me the drugs cheaper than to anybody else, and a few cents mean so much just now. Hark! (*Distant thunder.*) I must make haste before the storm is here. (*Exit D. in F.*)

STAUNTON (*calling from within*). Helen! Helen! It's here again. Priscilla, why will you torment me so! (*He*

enters, R., *half awake, supporting himself feebly on chairs and tables as he moves*.) Helen! Helen! Priscilla!
(*Enter* PRISCILLA, D. *in* F.)
PRIS. Who calls? What is it? ·
STAUNT. (*starting as he sees her*). Priscilla!
PRIS. How do you know me by name?
STAUNT. (*trembling*, R.). Priscilla!
PRIS. Why, is it, can it be, Philip Staunton? (*Down* C.)
STAUNT. (*gazing at her wildly*). Why do you haunt me so, Priscilla? I cannot drop off to sleep but I dream of you. I wake, and you are by my pillow. Is it because you know I am dying that you dog my steps?
PRIS. (*aside*). Ill — aged — wandering in mind! Can this be Philip Staunton? (*Aloud*.) Why, Philip, we have not met these twenty years, you and I.
STAUNT. Do you think to draw it out of me with those eyes of yours, Priscilla? Why will you not let me die in peace?
PRIS. (*soothingly*). Sit down, Philip. Come, let me make you comfortable in this big chair. There. And where shall I find a pillow for your back? In the next room? (*Exit into bed-chamber*, R.)
STAUNT. (*going* L.). Die in peace. If only she would let me die in peace! (*Sits* L.)
(*Enter* PRIS. R.)
PRIS. (*to* L., *arranging the pillow*). There. And now let me fan you. Your head is hot. Feel how cool my hands are.
STAUNT. Is it really you, Priscilla?
PRIS. Really I. (*Sits near him*.)
STAUNT. (*coming to himself*). I am afraid I was only half awake when I first came in. I had been dreaming. Do you ever dream, Priscilla?
PRIS. (*sighing*). Yes, Philip.
STAUNT. They are ugly things, these dreams, and when you are ill and weak, Priscilla, how all the faces of those you have injured in your life rise up before you.
PRIS. I don't know, Philip. I never wilfully injured any living being; nor you either, I trust.
STAUNT. (*roused*). Wilfully? Who said anything about wilfully? Of course no one injures a friend wilfully; it's because one is tempted; because one's blood is hot; because to own anything so sweet and bewildering as a young girl

one is willing to go through — Why do you listen to me so intently, Priscilla? Don't mind what I say. I'm ill. I'm an old man, Priscilla, an old man.

PRIS.   Only sixty, Philip.

STAUNT.   Two and twenty years between us.   I left you a girl of eighteen.

PRIS.   The girl of eighteen is now a woman of eight and thirty.

STAUNT.   No, no, Priscilla, don't ask me to believe that ; and why do you wear black? I always think of you in white, with a spray of lilacs in your belt. Where are your sisters?

PRIS.   Dead.

STAUNT.   And the old place?

PRIS.   Gone.   Everything is gone.   I am a poor woman now.

STAUNT.   I might have known you were poor to come here.   When did you come?

PRIS.   Last evening.

STAUNT.   And you — you never married?

PRIS.   I never married.

STAUNT.   And — John Masters?

PRIS.   John Masters and I have not met for twenty years.

STAUNT.   Not since the night —

PRIS. (*rising and going to* R., *agitated*).   Not since the night —

STAUNT. (*hastily*).   You mustn't mind anything you have heard me say, Priscilla. I'm ill. I'm not long for this world. I want Helen to love her father's memory, and if she should fancy —

PRIS.   Helen?

STAUNT.   My daughter.   I married soon after you sent me away, Priscilla. She's dead now, Beatrice, my wife ; but Helen — Ah, there she is now !

(*Enter* HEL., D. L. *in* F.)

HEL.   Why, father !   (*Down* L. *to him.*)

PRIS. (*to* C.).   An old friend of your father's. I heard him calling, and stepped in. I am lodging here now. My room is just next.

HEL.   Oh, how can I thank you ! Did you want me, father? I was longer than I meant to be.

STAUNT.   Oh, I was well cared for, Helen, well cared for.

PRIS.   She does not look like you, Philip.

STAUNT. No, thank fortune, there's not much of me in her.

PRIS. We must learn to know each other. I knew your father when I was a girl of eighteen and he the most fearless rider and best dancer in the county.

STAUNT. And now look at us. I gray and broken, and you slight and graceful still as a girl. Well, well.

PRIS. (*to* HELEN). Why do you look at me so wistfully? (*She takes* HELEN'S *hand.*)

HEL. Your eyes make me think of mamma's. I have no mother, you know.

PRIS. (*putting her arm around* HELEN). Poor child.

STAUNT. (*aside*). So Helen notices it. too. It was Beatrice's likeness to Priscilla that drew me to her.

HEL. May I bring my work sometimes and sit with you?

PRIS. (*kissing her*). The oftener the better, dear.

HEL. And you will tell me all about father when you used to know him. Did you know mamma, too?

PRIS. No, I never saw your mother. But now I must go. I shall expect you at my door very soon. Good-morning, Philip. Your little Helen and I are going to be fast friends.

STAUNT. Good-morning.

HEL. Good-morning, and thank you so much. (*Exit* PRIS. D. L. *in* F.) Father, who is she? What lovely eyes · and hair, and hasn't she a sweet voice? But why does she look so sad? I think I never saw so sad a face.

STAUNT. (*irritated*). No sadder than most faces; and when a woman has lost her parents and brothers and sisters and — and a handsome fortune, she has a right to look sad, hasn't she?

HEL. What! is she poor too? (C.)

STAUNT. Do you think she would come and lodge here if she were not? But there, there, my little girl, don't indulge in foolish fancies about people's being sad. Come here and tell your old dad you love him.

HEL. Dearest, dearest father.

STAUNT. A disreputable, battered old hulk, but you cherish a lingering fondness for him? Eh?

HEL. I wouldn't have you a bit different for all the world.

STAUNT. (*caressing her*). Your mother wanted a boy, but from the first moment you were put into my arms I knew you were to be the blessing of my life. A man doesn't often love two women as passionately as I have loved you and — and —

HEL. And mamma.

STAUNT. (*changing his tone*). Of course — your — mother, Helen.

HEL. Father, dear — (*She feels in his vest pocket.*)

STAUNT. What are you fumbling for in my pocket?

HEL. The key of the secretary.

STAUNT. What do you want out of the secretary?

HEL. Just a little money, dearest.

STAUNT. There's no money there.

HEL. I know it, but there's one more letter still of your autograph collection.

STAUNT. You don't mean to say the one hundred we raised on the last is all gone !

HEL. Oh, no — not all gone yet. (*Aside.*) He must not suspect how nearly.

STAUNT. There are no more letters. That was the last. Valuable autographs of Clay, Hamilton, Washington, Macaulay — all gone to pay for board and lodging in this vile rat-hole ! Pah !

HEL. Oh, but there is one more letter.

STAUNT. Whose?

HEL. It had slipped down behind a drawer. It's not mounted like the others. It was signed Priscilla.

STAUNT. (*starting*). Priscilla!

HEL. Is it from Priscilla, the Puritan maiden, father, to John Alden ?

STAUNT. Open the window. This room is stifling. Give me a glass of water. (HELEN *does so.*) There, there !

HEL. It's the thunder in the air. A storm is brewing.

STAUNT. (*aside*). Fool that I have been not to destroy it years ago. (*Aloud.*) Helen, how often must I tell you that my private papers are not to be disturbed ?

HEL. But, father, your autograph letters — you always let me read your autograph letters.

STAUNT. (*agitated*). What ? You read this —

HEL. No, I didn't happen to, father, but I might have.

STAUNT. It's a most dangerous habit, this reading other people's letters.

HEL. But an autograph letter —

STAUNT. A valuable autograph letter especially. It wears them out. Helen, I am very much displeased with you.

HEL. I am very sorry, father. I suppose it is exceedingly valuable. From Priscilla, you said. To John Alden ?

STAUNT. Of course. What other Priscilla could there be, whose autograph letter I should be likely to have. Certainly — Priscilla to John Alden. (*Aside.*) I'll destroy it this very day.

HEL. (*to table*, R. ; *aside*). How disturbed he looks! The slightest thing puts him into a fever. Poor father! (*Mixes drops.*) Here, father, it's time for your drops. (*To* L.)

STAUNT. Remember, Helen, that my private papers are not to be interfered with.

HEL. No, father. (*Aside.*) Oh, dear! Dr. Procter warned me he was not to be disturbed or excited. If only he can sleep now!

STAUNT. Drugs. Why do you give drugs to a dying man?

HEL. You are better, father, — oh, so much stronger and better. And now won't you try and sleep?

STAUNT. I hate sleep! Sleep is well enough for young things like you, Helen, but for us! Why, when we give ourselves up to sleep, it's like going bound into a tiger's cage, and all the jeering, snarling faces press close about, and one so powerless to lift a finger! Sleep! I hate sleep!

HEL. Oh, poor father! is it so bad as that! (*Aside.*) He's worse. I must quiet him. (*Aloud.*) Come, dear; the other room is cooler.

STAUNT. Why are you always shifting me about? Well, well! I spoiled you; I always did. (*She helps him to rise.*) But you love your old dad? There, there — (*Exeunt* D. R., HELEN *supporting* STAUNTON. *A knock. Enter* HAL D. *in* F., *with wine, fruit, and flowers.*)

HAL. Did some one say come in? No, no one did. Well, I'll just leave this wine (*to table*, R. *Pulls out two bottles of wine and puts them on table*) and this fruit and these white lilacs. I wonder if she'll think the lilacs are for her father?

(*Enter* MRS. G., D. *in* F.)

MRS. G. Oh, there you are. (*Aside.*) Fruit and flowers. Hm — and she said he wasn't keepin' company. (*Aloud.*) You're just the person I wanted to see. (*Down* C.)

HAL. (*aside*). I promised I wouldn't. (*Aloud.*) Oh, certainly, Mrs. Griggs. Quite at your service. You don't mind scarlet fever, of course.

MRS. G. Scarlet fever!

HAL. Seventeen cases at the hospital — but, as I said before —

MRS. G.   Out of this house, sir.   (*Draws back skirts.*)

HAL.   But you wished to see me.

MRS. G.   Do you want to scare all my lodgers away?
The sooner you leave these premises —

HAL.   Oh, very well.   Good-morning.   (*Exit* D. *in* F.)

HEL. (*enters* R.).   I thought I heard talking —   Oh, Mrs.
Griggs —

MRS. G.   Of all rash, reckless —   Well, Miss Helen, how
about the rent?

HEL.   Please speak softly.   My father is just falling
asleep —

MRS. G.   Haven't I been speakin' softly for five months?

HEL.   I know we are behindhand, but my father's illness
— all the necessary expenses —

MRS. G. (*going to door, speaks to* SHERIFF *outside*).   Just
step this way, will you?

(*Enter* SHERIFF, D. *in* F.)

SHERIFF (L.).   This is a disagreeable duty, miss.

HEL.   What do you mean?

MRS. G.   Oh, yes.   I wonder what he can mean?

SHERIFF.   I am ordered to eject you.

HEL.   Eject us!

MRS. G.   In plain English, you are to pack — bag and
baggage.

HEL.   But we can't —   My father is ill —

MRS. G.   That's your lookout.

HEL.   It would kill him to move.

MRS. G.   Then pay up.

SHERIFF (*to* MRS. G.).   Come now, I wouldn't be too hard
on her.

MRS. G.   That's none of your business.   Go ahead, go
ahead.   The furniture in this room is mine, but their things
is in the next room.   That door there.

SHERIFF (*moving towards door*, R.).   Very sorry, miss.

HEL. (*barring the door*).   You sha'n't go in.

SHERIFF.   Oh, come now.

MRS. G.   Go ahead.   It's only a trick.

HEL.   My father is ill — it may be dying.   The physician
said any excitement would be fatal.   We have no money —
here — take all we have —   (*Opens purse.*)   A few dollars —
the rest went this morning for medicine.   If you have a heart
in your bosom, take pity on us.

SHERIFF.   I don't like this business.

MRS. G. (*to* SHERIFF). She's rich friends. She could get the money easy as nothing. Go ahead.

SHERIFF (*pushing* HELEN *aside, and taking hold of the handle of the chamber door*). Law's law, miss. (*A peal of thunder.*)

HEL. (*seizing his arm*). Hear that crash! You cannot be so cruel as to thrust us out into the storm. (*It grows darker.*) Oh, if you have wife or children at home, have mercy on us.

SHERIFF. 'Tain't me ; it's the law.

HEL. Stand back !

SHERIFF. The law.

HEL. Stand back, I say ! She shall be paid, that harpy there. Leave the room, both of you ! Don't you hear me say she shall be paid ?

SHERIFF. Well, now, that sounds like business.

MRS. G. Didn't I tell you she could if she'd a mind to !

HEL. Give me one hour and you shall have your money.

Mrs. G. Nothin' like a good scare to —

HEL. Not another word. Leave the room, both of you. In an hour you shall be paid.

SHERIFF. I'm just as well pleased to be out of this.

MRS. G. Don't you budge out of the house till I get my grip on my rent. Come into the settin'-room and have a cup of tea.

(*Exeunt* SHERIFF *and* MRS. G., D. *in* F.)

HEL. That valuable autograph letter. I can raise something on that ; or, if that fails, my pride to the winds, and I will borrow of Hal. But how to get the key of the secretary without waking father! (*Opens chamber door*, R., *and looks in.*) Fast asleep. He must be fast asleep not to have heard their hateful voices. (*Exit into bed-chamber. Returns with key.*) Poor father, he did not feel me take the key from his pocket. (*Goes to secretary and unlocks it. Takes out papers.*) Ah, here it is, yellow with age. Priscilla. That's it. Now I'll ask that old friend of father's if she will be within call in case he wakes. I wonder what her name is. Thunder again ! I must hurry into my dress. Poor father! (*Exit*, D. *in* F., *as curtain falls.*)

ACT II.

Scene. —*Library at* John Masters's. *Doors* R., L., *and* C.
Books and pictures ad libitum. Enter, as curtain rises,
Hal. c., *with a bottle of wine under each arm, followed*
by Aunt Libby.

Aunt L.　It's not the port I object to, Hal; it's your
principles. (*Down* L.)

Hal.　Oh, my principles are quite as excellent as the port,
Aunt Libby. (C.)

Aunt L.　This is the second pair of bottles I've seen you
carrying up the cellar stairs to-day, as carefully as if they
were twins.

Hal.　Rather ancient, cobwebby twins. What's their
age? (*Examines label.*) 1840 seems to be the date of
birth.

Aunt L.　With all your faults, Hal, I never expected to
see you fill a drunkard's grave.

Hal.　Gracious, Aunt Libby! you don't expect I'm going
to drink all this myself, do you?

Aunt L.　Who is to drink it, I should like to know?

Hal.　A friend.

Aunt L.　A pretty kind of friend indeed.

Hal.　You are right there, Aunt Libby.

Aunt L.　I can fancy just what kind of a friend it is.

Hal.　I doubt it. (*Goes* R.)

Aunt L.　And how your friend will look when you appear
laden with this intoxicating gift. (*To* C.)

Hal.　So can I. (*Pursuing his own train of thought.*)

Aunt L. (*paying no attention to him*).　It must be that
red-nosed young man called Sparks.

Hal.　How her eyes will shine — but she'll shake her
head and look reproachful.

Aunt L. (*paying no attention to* Hal).　I can picture
his trembling hand, his blood-shot eyes —

Hal. (*pursuing his own reflections*).　The pretty flush on
her cheeks —

AUNT L. The almost purple hue of his nose. Hal, can you justify it to your conscience to make your friend's nose any redder than it already is?

HAL. Helen's nose red? Aunt Libby, what are you —

AUNT L. Helen? Who is Helen?

HAL. Oh! I did rather let the cat out of the bag that time, didn't I?

AUNT L. I insist on knowing who Helen is.

HAL. Well, then, Aunt Libby, it's to Helen I'm carrying this wine.

AUNT L. Goodness gracious! What would your Uncle John say?

HAL. If he could once see her. he'd be doing it himself.

AUNT L. Your Uncle John going about carrying bottles of wine to women called Helen! If she drinks all this, she will develop as red a nose as your friend Sparks. (*To* L.)

HAL (*hotly, to* C.). Excuse me, Aunt Libby, but it seems to me you are taking unwarrantable liberties with the noses of my friends. I —

AUNT L. A nose is a surer index of character than an eye, except, indeed, a black eye, which tells its own tale, and which your friend Sparks also possesses.

HAL. As for Miss Helen Staunton's nose, I cannot allow any one to mention it except in terms of the highest respect; and Sparks, poor Sparks; considering he is the one Prohibitionist of our set, I think it's rather hard you should be designing him for a drunkard's grave.

AUNT L. Don't try to make me believe Mr. Sparks is a teetotaler.

HAL. He plays on the eleven. It's all sunburn. But where's Uncle John?

AUNT L. I want you first to tell me about the young woman.

HAL. Well, Aunt Libby, it's a case of illness. The young lady's father is a convalescent. The port is for him.

AUNT L. (*to him*, C.). Why didn't you say so before, Henry? Convalescent? Now wouldn't he enjoy a little blanc-mange or calves'-foot jelly or —

HAL. I'm sure he would.

AUNT L. None of your skim-milk blanc-mange, but made with real cream and blanched almonds, according to my grandmother's recipe.

HAL. Aunt Libby, you are a jewel!

AUNT L.   And some calves'-foot jelly.   The young people
of the present day have not the first notion of genuine calves'-
foot jelly.   And how about a little delicate sponge cake to
go with it?   What do the physicians nowadays say about
sponge cake?   In my day they used to recommend it.

HAL (*aside*).   It won't do not to appear to know.   (*Aloud.*)
Well, Aunt Libby, physicians differ as to sponge cake.   As
the celebrated Dr. Rosicrucius says, "Sponge cake, like other
porous and vascular bodies, is prone, when infiltrated with
aqueous or other fluids, to take on a certain turgescent,
bulbous, hypertrophied form, often oppressive to other organs
contiguous to the digestive system."

AUNT L.   You don't say!   Then you wouldn't advise my
sending any?

HAL.   On the contrary, I should advise sending one of
your largest loaves.   (*Aside.*)   Helen can eat it, if her father
can't.

AUNT L.   Well, I'll go and start things.   Just run down
to the cellar, Hal, and bring up a bottle of Sicily Madeira.
Here are the keys.

HAL.   All right.   (*Exeunt* HAL, R., *and* AUNT L., C.)
(*Enter*, L, JOHN MASTERS.   *He wears a shade over his eyes.*)

MAST.   Another day of this and I shall go wild.   A deaf
man at a concert derives as much pleasure from the music
as I in my library from my books.   Here I am surrounded
by them — good friends, the best of friends ever a man could
have, his books — and not a word can I get out of one of them.

(*Enter* AUNT LIBBY, C.)

AUNT L. (R.).   Oh, John dear, here you are.   I was just
setting about my blanc-mange when I remembered this was
the time for your drops.

MAST. (C.).   Confound the drops!

AUNT L.   Where's the bottle?   Oh, here.   (*Table*, R.)
How are your eyes?

MAST.   Worse every time you put that nasty fluid into
them.   (*Sits*, L.)

AUNT L.   Oh, no, my dear, oh, no!   Don't be childish,
John, and peevish.   (*Goes to him.*)   Come, let me put the
drops in, and then I'll read the morning news.   Let me take
the shade off.   Now, put your head back.

MAST. (*submitting resignedly*).   Where's Hal?

AUNT L.   In the cellar.   Now, my dear John, considering

you yourself, by disobeying orders and not following my advice, have brought this trouble on —

MAST. Augh!

AUNT L. What's the matter?

MAST. It went into my ear.

AUNT L. For you cannot deny that, if I warned you once, I warned you fifty —

MAST. My nose!

AUNT L. — times, but you would pay no attention, and consequently —

MAST. I won't have the blinder on again.

AUNT L. But, my dear John!

MAST. Through?

AUNT L. With the drops, yes —

MAST. And the advice too?

AUNT L. No, indeed; I've only just begun. (MASTERS *sighs*.) That fine print — those horrid, old foreign books you pore over, and those letters in such disagreeable crabbed handwritings — if only you would confine yourself to large print now for the future, I am sure you would have no more trouble with your eyes. Why, for the whole winter I've been going through all of Buckminster's sermons merely because they happen to be in such beautiful large print. Why don't you say anything? You haven't gone to sleep, have you?

MAST. As if it were possible, Libby, to go to sleep while you are talking. I thought you said something about the newspaper.

AUNT L. Oh, yes, — the paper. (*To* C., *sits*.) Now, here's the advertising column. Letters one quarter of an inch long, and really quite interesting and improving to the mind too. "Whole chamber sets for thirty to forty dollars upwards, of choice workmanship, elegant in designs and dainty in details, fitted to adorn" —

MAST. Good heavens, Libby! I'm not a young sprig about to get married and set up housekeeping.

AUNT L. Well, well. What do you want? (*Looks through paper*.) President's message — hm—m — foreign news — hm—m — elopement — tck-tck-tck — a war somewhere in Africa — but those names are so very queer — bill passed the legislature — that doesn't look interesting — a fire — there's always a fire — man murders his wife — I can't endure murders — such bad taste. I don't see what you men find in the newspaper anyway.

MAST. (*with closed eyes*). What's Hal doing in the cellar?

AUNT L. Oh, here's something interesting —

MAST. (*sitting up*). What?

AUNT L. Black satin coming into .fashion again, so my old satin gown —

MAST. (*relapsing*). It seems to me Hal's a precious long time in the cellar.

AUNT L. Oh, here's something else. John, isn't it dread'ul?

MAST. What?

AUNT L. Large district devoted to buckwheat flooded — and Hal is so fond of buckwheat cakes for breakfast, though the amount of maple syrup he pours over them is enough to ruin his digestion, for —

MAST. What's Hal doing in the cellar anyway?

AUNT L. Oh, getting me some Sicily Madeira. Hm—m (*looking through paper*) — nothing else — really nothing. By the way. Walsingham — Walsingham — Let me see, that's the name of that queer man in baggy trousers and green spectacles, isn't it, that comes and brings you those dreadful old books?

MAST. I don't remember about his trousers, but he owns the rarest Aldine Aristotle in the country. What does it say about Walsingham?

AUNT L. Oh. nothing — merely that since acquiring the Brenton collection of autograph letters —

MAST. (*starting up*). The Brenton collection! Walsingham acquired the Brenton collection!

AUNT L. (*reading*). " Mr. Walsingham has now probably the most valuable collection of autograph letters in private hands."

MAST. How did he come by them? Where did he run across them? What did he pay? What else does it say?

AUNT L. Why, how excited you get over trifles, John; and black satin might go in and out of fashion twenty times a year, and you wouldn't wink. That's all about Mr. Walsingham.

MAST. Walsingham's a lucky fellow.

(*Enter* HAL, R.)

HAL. I put your wine in the pantry, Aunt Libby.

AUNT L. (*rising*). Hal, I'll leave you to entertain your uncle now. I've read all there was of any interest in the newspaper. On the pantry shelf, you said? (*Exit* C. D.)

HAL (*to* C.). Well, Uncle John, how goes it?

MAST. Oh, tolerably, except for the eye water. It puts me back every time.

HAL. Where women and medicine are concerned, Uncle John, you are a perfect old cynic.

MAST. I've tried both —

HAL. And survived both, so you see neither is fatal. (*Hesitatingly.*) Uncle John —

MAST. Yes.

HAL (*taking another chair*, R.). Uncle John —

MAST. Well.

HAL (*rising again ; to* C.). Uncle John —

MAST. Good Lord, Hal ! has it come to this?

HAL. To what?

MAST. Doesn't the mere fact that you are incapable of looking me in the eye prove to you that you are doing something you ought to be ashamed of?

HAL. I'm not ashamed of it.

MAST. Then out with it. After all, you are more to be pitied than blamed. First mumps — then measles — then scarlet fever — then hobbledehoyism — then — out with it, Hal. Who is she? (*Rises.*)

HAL. It's impossible to talk to you, Uncle John, after this. You — you — take all the poetry out of it.

MAST. I've only been doing what Father Time will sooner or later. (*To* R.)

HAL. Not in my case. (*Sits*, C.)

MAST. It's all very pretty, Hal, at your age, I know. It's like looking at the dew on the meadow grass in the morning from the vantage ground of the gravel path ; but leave the gravel path and brush through the dew, and you find it mighty nasty walking.

HAL. I knew your opinion of women, Uncle John, but I did not think you'd make it so hard for me.

MAST. Hard ! I wish some one had tried to make it hard for me. It would have been easier afterwards. But there, my boy, sit down. I'll listen to you. Only don't dwell too rapturously on her perfections — I'll listen to you.

HAL. Uncle John, I know I owe you everything from the time I was so high, but a word of sympathy at this crisis would be worth all you have done for me twice over.

MAST. (*aside*). Poor boy ! (*Aloud.*) Sympathize? I

do sympathize with you profoundly, Hal. You are a case
for sympathy.

HAL (*starting up*). No, I'm 'not a case for sympathy.
You ought to wish me joy! It's the highest, most over-
whelming thing that could come to a man — to love any one
as pure and sweet and beautiful as Helen! But why do I
talk? You don't know anything about it! (*To* L.)

MAST. (*taking out a cigarette*). So her name is Helen!
(*Aside.*) Poor boy! The greater the rapture now, the
deeper the after disappointment. (*Sits,* R.)

HAL (*to* C.). I was coming to you with a plan. I had
meant to say, "Uncle John, you have done everything for
me" —·

MAST. That's not worth talking about. Got a match?

HAL (*giving him one*). You have put me through Exe-
ter and Harvard, you are footing my bills at the Medical
School —

MAST. Well, sir, if I choose to, what concern is it of
yours?

HAL. You even intended sending me to Vienna for two
years, to finish my medical course.

MAST. Say intend, not intended.

HAL. No, intended, Uncle John, for that's all past. What
I meant to ask was that you would lend me half the sum all
this would cost, and let me leave my profession and take a
clerkship. In a year I should be earning enough to sup-
port —

MAST. A wife and family. Oh, you young fools, you
young fools!

HAL. Uncle John —

MAST. And to think I pulled you through the scarlet
fever for this!

HAL. I say I *did* intend asking you this, but now — now
that you have said such things of Helen —

MAST. What in the devil's name have I said against
Helen?

HAL. You insisted that *she* was not worth the paltry sacrifice of my profession.

MAST. O Hal, Hal! As if there were a woman in the
world worth the sacrifice of a cigarette.

HAL. You never saw Helen.

MAST. I never want to.

HAL. So gentle, so sweet, so noble —

MAST. Spare me, Hal. (*Rising.*)

HAL. If I spare you Helen, I'll spare you myself. Do you think I can go on taking your money while you insult the woman I love! I'll go this instant and look up some employment — I'll —

MAST. (*to* C., *taking him by the arm*). Hal, Hal! don't let a woman come between us. They are not worth it, my boy, they are not worth it.

HAL. One could see you had never been in love.

MAST. Never been in love! Never been in love! (*He moves away to* L., *and seats himself.*) Hal, come here. (*He speaks with an effort.*) Would my words come to you with more weight if I told you that I — Sit down, Hal. (*Pause;* HAL *sits,* L.) Hal, there was a woman once — there are none quite like her now. The rosebud freshness seems lacking in the young girls of nowadays.

HAL. Wait till you see Helen!

MAST. Such a voice. Hal — so gentle and caressing — and her eyes — you never dreamed of such eyes — and the proud, womanly curves of her lips, and then her hair — (*Laughs cynically.*) I beg your pardon, Hal; I did not mean to inflict all this on you.

HAL. Oh, go on. Everything you say just describes Helen.

MAST. Helen? Helen could no more compare with Priscilla than — there, there. I beg your pardon. I will stick to facts merely.

HAL. So her name was Priscilla?

MAST. Who told you that?

HAL. Why, you yourself, just now. Priscilla — I like the name.

MAST. I used to think it the divinest melody in the world; though, for the matter of that, I remember fancying that when she said " John," which is certainly not a remarkably euphonious name, that too was pure music.

HAL. I know just how it sounded. You ought to hear Helen say Hal. I made her one day.

MAST. Well, Hal, Priscilla and I were engaged.

HAL. You engaged!

MAST. Nine happy months we were engaged. I believed she loved me. She made me think so. Then came a lovers' quarrel.

HAL. Yes —

MAST.   It happened at a country ball.   I was jealous of the attentions of another man.   I left her in anger.   She was proud, and my last words were, let it all be over between us (*rises and moves* R.) — over between us.

HAL.   Poor Uncle John.

MAST. (*returning to* C.).   That night, after I had galloped home under the stars, I wrote her a wild letter.   I reproached her for my wasted love, but I implored her, if she ever had cared for me, to send me a word, a flower — the slightest token.   I waited in feverish pain.   Hours passed — days. Not a word.   The next thing I heard was that she was to be married to my rival.

HAL.   Heartless jilt!

MAST.   Let her rest in peace.

HAL.   And you — what did you do?

MAST.   I took the next steamer for Germany.   Life abroad suited me.   I stayed ten years.   Then my sister Mary, your mother, died, and I came back and took you.

HAL.   And Priscilla?

MAST.   For years, I never let any one mention her name to me.   All I know is that the man she chose is now a widower.   When or where she died I never heard.   I have lived buried in my books, as you know.

HAL. (*aside*).   Poor Uncle John!

MAST.   Now, Hal, take the word of a man who has been through this fever in the blood — who has lived it down and come out sane and safe.   You don't want to marry a pretty fool; you don't want to marry a sage in petticoats.   Woman is too light weight to carry both heart and head.   Your Aunt Libby has heart.   Priscilla had head, and I give her credit for that.

HAL.   Helen has both heart and head.

MAST.   Look at me.   What more should I want?   I have my books, my pipe, my fire, your Aunt Libby to order my meals, and you to turn off my superfluous advice upon. Stick to your profession, Hal; and if, as you grow gray, you crave young blood about you, take to your heart some young rascal as I took you, through with his teething and squalling, and unencumbered by a mother; and may he turn out a comfortable nuisance to you as you were to me, before this Helen of Troy lit the torches of war in our peaceful citadel.

HAL. (*rises*).   Uncle John, if you could but see her!

(*Enter* AUNT LIBBY, C. D.)

AUNT L. John, come — change your coat — quick!

MAST. Why, in Heaven's name?

AUNT L. (*down* R.) There's a young girl asking to see you.

MAST. This coat is quite good enough for any young girl in creation.

AUNT L. I insist, John, on your changing your coat. This is frayed around the button-holes; and what reports would be carried abroad if I let you appear like this, I cannot say. Come! She's taking off her waterproof in the passage. Come!

MAST. (*going* R.). If you only realized, Libby, how much more comfortable a frayed coat was than a whole one.

(*Exeunt* AUNT L. *and* MAST., R. *Enter* MAID. C. D.)

MAID. This way, miss. Mr. Masters will be right in.

(*Enter* HELEN, C. D.; *exit* MAID.)

HEL. (*aside*). What a delightful house! (*Perceives* HAL.) Oh, Mr. Masters!

HAL (*rising*, L.). Helen! Miss Staunton!

HEL. (*aside*, C.). Oh, dear! I hoped he would be at the Medical School.

HAL (*to* C., *ecstatically*). You needed something? You came to see me?

HEL. I came to see your uncle.

HAL (*taken aback*). Uncle John! But I thought you didn't know him.

HEL. Would you mind, please — I — I — should like to see him alone.

HAL. Alone!

HEL. Yes, alone.

HAL (*aside*). What can she want to see him alone for?

HEL. I think I hear him coming.

HAL (*aside*). She seems very anxious to get rid of me. She doesn't mention the lilacs I left for her. (*Stiffly.*) Oh, certainly; I'll not force myself upon you. Good-morning.

HEL. Good-morning. (*Exit* HAL, L.) Foolish boy! (*Enter* MASTERS, R.; *aside.*) So this is Hal's Uncle John.

MAST. (R.). Oh, good-morning. You wanted to see me?

HEL. I came here from Mr. Walsingham's.

MAST. Ah!

HEL. I went there to show him a valuable autograph letter. His son told me his father was away, but spoke of you as also being interested in such matters.

MAST. Yes.

HEL. (*aside*). How stiff and ungetatable Hal's Uncle John is. (*Aloud.*) Mr. Walsingham has, at different times, purchased autograph letters from my father. My father owned part of the celebrated Brenton collection.

MAST. (*interested*). The Brenton collection? Indeed! So it was of your father Mr. Walsingham purchased the Brenton collection?

HEL. I have here the last letter of that collection.

MAST. (*to* C.). Oh, indeed! indeed! Where is it? Allow me to look at it. Ah — my eyes — that confounded — I beg your pardon — that unfortunate eye-wash. It makes everything a blur.

HEL. The letter is one from Priscilla to John Alden.

MAST. (*excited*). No, really! That is indeed a priceless autograph! Let me see it. (HELEN *hands letter.*) But what a careless way to treat so valuable a document!

HEL. Most of the letters were mounted, of course; but this one never was.

MAST. (*aside*). That confounded eye-wash! I can make out nothing but yellow note-paper and a faint scrawl. (*Aloud.*) Of course, belonging to the Brenton collection, the genuineness of this autograph cannot be questioned. Might I trouble you to read it to me?

HEL. Oh, certainly, if I can. The handwriting is faint. (*Opens letter.*) Ah!

MAST. What is it?

HEL. (*stooping*). Why, this fell out. Look! A pressed flower — a white lilac!

MAST. Let me see.

HEL. To think of its lying all these years in this letter. It's still sweet.

MAST. What is the date?

HEL. It's not dated at all.

MAST. (*impatiently*). Just like a woman!

HEL. There's no heading either. (*Reading.*) "You beg me for the slightest token — a flower, a word — to tell you I once loved you. Here is a sprig of white lilac. I reach from my window to pull it, all dewy wet. I have kissed it a hundred times, but the word — O John, John, an ocean of words could not bear you my love, my longing, my agony of soul!"

MAST. That's no language of two hundred years ago!

HEL. Did Puritan maidens write like this?

MAST. You say the letter belonged to the Brenton collection. This is no Puritan maiden. But go on — go on.

HEL. (*reading*). "All night I have sat at my window, and now the sun is rising behind the pines on Randolph Hill —"

MAST. (*starting*). Randolph Hill! (*To* L.)

HEL. Yes, Randolph Hill. I'm sure it's Randolph Hill.

MAST. Go on.

HEL. "It strikes the elm at the foot of the lawn, where you and I have sat every day together hand in hand."

MAST. (*dreamily*). "Where you and I have sat every day together hand in hand." (*Aside.*) The old, old story.

HEL. (*reading*). "O John, the torture of this night has changed me from the shy girl who trembled at your passionate kisses to a woman conscious that without you life would be as day without its sun, as night without its stars! Time after time since we parted have I gone over the terrible night: the glitter, the whirl of the ball-room — your jealous eyes — Philip's unsought attentions —"

MAST. (*starting*). Philip? Not Philip! It cannot be Philip!

HEL. But it is. Look for yourself. Oh, I forgot.

MAST. (*sitting down*, L.). Of course; why mightn't it be Philip? But Randolph Hill, and the elm at the foot of the lawn, and Philip. Go on, go on.

HEL. (*reading*). "Then the hurried parting on the porch — your words, 'Let all be over between us.' Your riding away under the stars — my bursting heart — the hateful mockery of the gay music within —"

MAST. (*rising and striding to* HELEN, C.). What, in Heaven's name, are you inventing there?

HEL. It's all as I read it —

MAST. (*looking over*). Go on — where are you? "Mockery of the gay music —" Oh, to be able to see! Go on, I say.

HEL. (*reading*). "I look at the little ring you gave me, and it whispers hope — the little ring with the motto that only you and I know —"

MAST. (*violently agitated*).   " That only you and I know."
Go on, child, go on.

HEL.   It's blurred here — perhaps by a tear.

MAST.   For God's sake, go on !

HEL.   It's in quotation marks.   It is the motto itself.   It
looks like, " To love — is — to love is —

MAST.   " To love is to trust."

HEL.   That's it — " To love is to trust."   How did you
know ?

MAST. (*seizing the letter*).   To love is to trust — and
signed, you say — how is it signed ?

HEL.   Priscilla.

MAST.   How, in Heaven's name, did you come by this ?

HEL.   It was among my father's papers.

MAST.   Your father's name ?

HEL.   Philip Staunton.

MAST.   Philip Staunton !   Philip Staunton !   How came
he by the letter ?   Why did I never receive it ?   What
treachery !   O Priscilla !   Priscilla !   My lost love !   God
help us !   Priscilla !

HEL. (*aside*).   What can it all mean ?   What have I done ?

MAST.   Take me to your father — Philip Staunton, you
say.   Oh, my lost love !   Priscilla !   Priscilla !

CURTAIN.

ACT III.

SCENE.— STAUNTON'S *room again. Same as before.* HAL'S *lilacs on window-sill, up* R.

STAUNT. (*appearing from chamber,* R.) Now to destroy that letter. Madness to have kept it all these years! Madness to have tried to make myself believe I would ever deliver it! And now I am dying. Too late, too late! and I cannot leave it to fall into Helen's hands. (*Up* R.) Why, how heavy the air is. (*At window.*) I could swear I smelt white lilacs. No, no; it was seeing Priscilla that made me think of white lilacs. But yet — ah! I was not mistaken — there are white lilacs. Who could have brought them? (*Takes up spray and smells it.*) How pale she was that morning, and her eyes like a wild thing, and all about us the still morning air heavy with the scent of white lilacs I hate the flower. (*Throws down the spray.*) But the letter — the letter. (*To secretary.*) Where is my key? I had it this morning. Helen asked me for it, but I refused. I refused, I remember. She had seen the letter. If she knew what it contained! Why, where can the key be? Perhaps I can force the lock. (*Tries to pry open the secretary.*) Alas! my feeble hands! Oh, the misery of being old and ill!

(*Enter* MRS. G., D. L. *in* F., *peering in.*)

MRS. G. Oh, I thought he was asleep. (*Retires and knocks loudly.*)

STAUNT. (*starting*). Come in.

MRS. G. Well, has your daughter brought the money yet? (*Down* L.)

STAUNT. What money?

MRS. G. What money indeed! The rent.

STAUNT. You dare to ask rent for this miserable rat-hole! (*Down* C.)

MRS. G. Oh, very well. March out of the old rat-hole if you don't like it.

STAUNT. Where is my daughter?

MRS. G. Gone to beg money of the young man that's keepin' company with her.

STAUNT. What do you mean?

MRS. G. I've been inquirin' about him. He's the nephew of that rich Mr. John Masters that lives in the old Masters house, on Chatterton Place.

STAUNT. Nephew of John Masters! Old Masters house, on Chatterton Place! Say that again — say that again.

MRS. G. No occasion. You repeated it all right. Now what I want to know is, does your daughter mean business, or don't she? The young man does, and if he marries her, he's only got to say to his uncle, "Give me another house as big as yours, and servants and horses and all," and his uncle'll do it. He just sets everything by that nephew.

STAUNT. (*aside, going* R.). Nephew to John Masters! Why didn't he tell me? Why didn't any one tell me? But I've been ill so long — I remember it was the day I fainted in the street, we first met the young man. He helped me home. I thought the name was Marston, not Masters. I liked the boy — a fine, manly fellow. And it was his photograph I caught Helen blushing over one day! So my little girl has found some one she loves better even than her father!

MRS. G. Muttering to himself as usual. Decidedly off. Well — I'll give her half an hour more. (*Exit*, D L *in* F.)

STAUNT. Well, well, it's best so; and I can die knowing she will be cared for. John Masters's nephew in love with my little girl! But the letter — the letter! It must be destroyed this instant. If it should fall into his hands. If he should discover that Helen's father was the man who — Oh, where is the key? (*Paces up and down.*) The key — the key! Oh, my head! The room swims! The window — air — air—the white lilacs — (*Falls fainting on a chair*, L.)

(*Enter* PRIS., D. L. *in* F.)

PRIS. Who called? Ah! (*Runs to* STAUNTON. *gives him water, etc.*) Poor Philip! poor Philip! and the air so close and sweet. Ah! white lilacs. (*Up* R. ; *opens window.*) But where can his daughter be this long time? She should not leave him like this. There, Philip, you are better now. (*Down* L.)

STAUNT. (*opening his eyes*). Priscilla!

PRIS. Why, of course it's Priscilla.

STAUNT. Take them away. (*Pointing to lilacs.*)

PRIS. I'll set them on the sill. They are too sweet for the house. (*She sets them outside the window.*)

STAUNT. Don't ask me, Priscilla — I can't tell you — I can't. It's all past and gone. Let bygones be bygones. Let me die in peace, Priscilla!

PRIS. (*stroking his hand*). Such a nice hand as you have, Philip. I always remembered your hand, so well formed and knit —

STAUNT. It's no use. Your eyes drag it out of me. It will not let me rest. Priscilla, I loved you as never man loved a woman. To the destruction of my own soul I loved you. You must hear me before I die.

PRIS. Come, come, Philip; these are sickly fancies — feverish dreams. Calm yourself, old friend.

STAUNT. That night twenty years ago, when John Masters and you parted in anger —

PRIS. Don't, Philip!

STAUNT. That early morning after the ball, when my restless love drove me wandering by your windows —

PRIS. For Heaven's sake, Philip, let the old times rest!

STAUNT. There you sat, pale as the white lilacs that scented the air all about. I can never smell white lilacs without picturing it. And when you saw me, "Philip," you cried, "oh, Philip," and I drew near, and stood beneath your window.

PRIS. (*covering her face*). Spare me, Philip.

STAUNT. Your eyes were wild with pain, Priscilla. I see them now. I have seen them ever since. "Philip," you cried, "for the love of God, carry this for me to — you know whom."

PRIS. (*rising and moving to* R.). "To you know whom."

STAUNT. Why did you choose me, Priscilla, to carry that fatal letter?

PRIS. I could not wait. The sun was barely risen — all the world was asleep but you and I. I fancied John too must be keeping watch.

STAUNT. Priscilla — that letter you gave me — that letter —

PRIS. O Philip, peace!

STAUNT. (*rising*). Can you not see — can you not read in my face, Priscilla, that the letter —

PRIS. (*coming near and seizing his arm*). Yes — Philip — the letter —

STAUNT. Never — reached (*his voice sinks*) — John — Masters's — hands. (PRIS. *stands a moment motionless gazing at him; then stretches out her arms with a wild gesture, turns and buries her face in her hands.*) I was wild for you, Priscilla. I worshipped your very shadow. How could I sit calmly by and let another win you! I knew you had quarrelled. I k..ew John's proud spirit. The devil in me whispered, "It lies in your hands to keep them apart. You loved her first. She would have learned to love you if he had not come between." I read the letter; I never delivered it. I lied when I told you that same day that I had. I lied when I let it come to John Masters's ears that you were to marry me! He left without seeing you again. Why don't y u speak to me, Priscilla? Priscilla, I loved you so! Speak to me, Priscilla.

PRIS. (*shuddering*). Be silent!

STAUNT. I loved you, Priscilla.

PRIS. (*starting up fiercely*). Don't speak to me of love!

STAUNT. Do you think I did not repent what I had done? In sackcloth and ashes repent it?

PRIS. He must be told.

STAUNT. Who?

PRIS. John Masters.

STAUNT. (*startled*). To what end? What could you gain? He has grown warped and hard, they say; bitter, and hates all women. What would you gain by making him curse my memory?

PRIS. Warped and hard? John, my John, warped and hard? And who brought this about? You! You, who made him believe I had forsaken him! You, who taught him to look upon woman's love as but a passing breath! (*To c.*)

STAUNT. You will not tell him!

PRIS. (*turning*). And all his life he has thought — yes, this very moment, while here I stand yearning, panting for a word from his lips, a touch of his hand — this very moment thinks of me as false!

STAUNT. Priscilla!

PRIS. But he shall know. O John! John! wherever you are, I shall find you. I —

STAUNT. Priscilla, listen!

PRIS. Oh, the bitter joy of it! Not scorned, not wilfully forsaken, as you led me to believe; trapped, deluded, treacherously torn from him. But he was true to me — oh, the bitter joy of it! — true, true, true! (*She buries her face in her hands.*)

STAUNT. (*aside*, L.). And this is what my coward conscience has led me into! Fool! Could I not have kept silent to the last? Could I not have remembered my child? My little Helen! What can she hope from John Masters now? John Masters permit his nephew to marry the daughter of the man who — (*Aloud.*) Where are you going, Priscilla? Don't leave me like this!

PRIS. What can you further want of me?

STAUNT. Priscilla, I have not long to live —

PRIS. Then make your peace with your God, if you can.

STAUNT. How hard at times even the gentlest woman can be! I go empty-handed, as I came into the world. I leave Helen penniless —

PRIS. She will marry.

STAUNT. She would have married the man she loves but for you.

PRIS. For me!

STAUNT. She loves John Masters's nephew.

PRIS. Mary's son?

STAUNT. Mary's son once; John's now. He adopted the boy. Will he be likely to give his consent to the marriage of his nephew to the child of one — who —

PRIS. And you dare ask me for this sacrifice? Me, whom you have so irreparably wronged!

STAUNT. But for a time, Priscilla — but for a time. Can you not wait till the sod is over my grave? When the young people are married, then go to him, if you will. Tell my daughter her father was a reprobate. Tell John Masters the father of his nephew's wife wrecked his life. John has grown bitter, they say, but he will not think it is because you are penniless that you come to him, and he a rich man; he will not think —

PRIS. Philip Staunton, beware!

STAUNT. Forgive me, Priscilla, but you will wait? Look at my shaking hand; it will not be for long. You will not wreck the happiness of a young girl who has never injured you, and whose only fault is in being of my blood.

PRIS. (*aside*). He is right. How could I go to John and say, " John, I was true to you — I am true to you. You are the only man I ever loved!" Oh, Heaven help me!

STAUNT. Listen. Priscilla. I will write a letter to John, I will tell him everything as it happened ; and after I am dead and Helen is married, she shall give it to him.

PRIS. You will do this?

STAUNT. I will, I swear I will ; but there is one condition. Helen must never know. She loves me — my little Helen — strange as it may seem to you. You will not break her heart by telling her that her father —

PRIS. Never, Philip! believe me. Helen's love for you shall not be disturbed by word of mine.

STAUNT. Ah, that is the old Priscilla. (*To* C.) Now give me your hand on our compact. You shrink back! It is a dying man implores you, Priscilla.

PRIS. (*taking his hand*). There, Philip.

STAUNT. I do not ask your forgiveness, merely your promise. You promise.

(D. L. *in* F. *is opened by* HELEN. MASTERS *stands behind her*.)

PRIS. I promise, Philip.

MAST. That voice ! Am I dreaming !

HEL. Father, I've brought a guest.

(PRIS. *turns and sees* MASTERS.)

PRIS. John!

MAST. My God ! Priscilla ! (*Down* C.)

PRIS. John! (*She lays her hand in his, then glides out of the room.* D. *in* F.)

HEL. (*following her*). Oh, I want to ask you — (*She joins* PRIS. *in the passage; and, taking her hand, appears to be talking earnestly with her.* MASTERS *stands* C., *gazing at them half dazed*.)

STAUNT. (L.) Masters.

MAST. (*turning on him fiercely*). Staunton !

STAUNT. Sit down, Masters, sit down.

MAST. In your house ! And you dare — (*Checking himself; aside*.) Gray and broken ! I came to fling his treachery in his face, but it is the face of a dead man ! And Priscilla alive !

STAUNT. You find me changed, Masters.

MAST. (*gazing at* PRISCILLA, *who has put her arm about* HELEN ; *aside*). Priscilla alive !

STAUNT But it matters less when we have **young shoots** about us. A fine boy, your nephew, Masters.

MAST. What! You know Hal ?

Staunt. Has he never spoken to you of us ?

Mast. Never.

Staunt. Never of Helen?

Mast. What is Helen to you?

Staunt. My daughter, Masters.

Mast. Your daughter! So that is Hal's Helen. Your daughter! Priscilla's daughter! And Priscilla alive ! How did it come to my ears that you were a widower, Staunton ? Priscilla's daughter!

Staunt. (*amazed*). Priscilla's daughter! Then you never heard— (*Checks himself; aside.*) So he fancies Priscilla my wife! He never heard of my marriage to Beatrice. Fancied the report of my wife's death referred to Priscilla! I have said nothing, nothing. It's all his own fancy. If he chooses to think Priscilla Helen's mother, am I responsible? He loved Priscilla; he would be drawn to Priscilla's daughter. He will find out his mistake soon enough without my telling him, but if before he finds it out I could gain his consent to the match! He always had Quixotic notions of honor. He would keep to his word even after he discovered he had been deceived —

Mast. (*aside*). Priscilla's daughter! and she did love me once. It was through treachery he won her. My Hal in love with Priscilla's daughter! But how came the girl with her mother's letter? And not knowing it was her mother's!

Staunt. You are no friend to marriage, I know, Masters ; but it makes a difference who a girl's mother is.

Mast. Yes, yes. (*Aside, going* R) Let me think. Could it have been that the girl found the letter among her father's papers, had heard of our broken· engagement, knew through Hal how averse I was to marriage, strove through subterfuge to soften me towards her mother, and through that towards herself?

(Priscilla *and* Helen *move out of sight.*)

Staunt. (*to* C.). You see, I speak of the girl's mother, not her father. There never was much love lost between you and me, John Masters. (*Goes slowly up and closes door*)

Mast. Little enough, Heaven knows ; and but for your wife's sake you should this moment answer for — (*Aside.*) I cannot strike a dying man, and *her* husband !

Staunt. (*down* C.). For my wife's sake, then, Masters, think of my child. She loves your boy. She has been a

devoted daughter to me. She will make him happy, as her
mother has made me. Do not be hard on them. Promise
me you will not stand in their way. (*Aside.*) I have said
nothing, nothing. If he draws his own conclusions from my
words, am I to blame?

MAST   This very morning I told Hal he was a young fool
to think of marriage.

STAUNT.   But you did not then know who Helen was.

MAST.   No, I did not know who Helen was, nor did I
know that her father — (*Checks himself; aside.*) Silence,
for the sake of Priscilla, who loves him!

STAUNT.   But now you do know, Masters, you will not
oppose them? Promise me, Masters — promise — us —

MAST.   What is a promise to you?

STAUNT.   You will help them?

MAST.   Help a child of yours? Tell me how much of
your false blood runs in her veins!

STAUNT.   Go on ; abuse a dying man. Masters ; it's gen-
erous. (*Aside.*) What does he suspect? (*Aloud.*) But
I'll bear it in silence As for Helen, she is all her mother.

MAST.   Well for her that she is.

STAUNT.   You'll stand by her, Masters, for her mother's
sake. Forget who her father was. You'll not break her
heart and your boy's? Your promise. (*To* R.) Your hand.

MAST. (*starting back*).   No, not my hand in the treacher-
ous palm that —

(*Enter* HELEN, D. *in* F.)

HEL.   Father!

STAUNT. (*aside*).   Who has told him? (*Aloud.*) Helen
— the key of my secretary. Where is it? (*To* L.)

HEL.   Here, father. I took it. Can I get anything for
you? (*At* C.)

STAUNT.   No, no, give it to me. (*Aside, taking key.*)
I'll destroy it this moment. (*Aloud.*) Run away now,
Helen, run away. (*He goes up to the desk.*)

MAST. (R.).   Come here, child.

STAUNT (*fumbling among his papers*).   Run away,
Helen, run away.

MAST. (*turning up her face between his hands*).   A frank
smile ; but not hers. Sweet eyes ; but not hers. Pure lips ;
but not hers.

HEL.   You mean my mother?

MAST.   Yes. I knew her at your age.

STAUNT. (*turning round, aghast*). Gone! Robbed! Who has been at my papers? (*Down* C.)

HEL. (*to* C.). What is it, father?

STAUNT. (*drawing her toward him and speaking in a hoarse whisper*). That letter — that valuable autograph letter!

HEL. (*soothingly*). The autograph letter is quite safe. Father dear, it is —

MAST. (*drawing out letter*). In the hands of its owner.

STAUNT. (*covering his face*). My God!

HEL. What does it all mean? What is the letter? What —

MAST. (*to* STAUNTON). Then she knows nothing?

STAUNT. (*groaning*). Nothing.

MAST. (*taking* HELEN'S *hand*, R. C.). The letter was mine. It was — lost. It came into your father's hands. Your father was keeping it — to return to me.

STAUNT. (*faintly*). Wine, Helen, wine! (*Sits* L.)

HEL. Yes, dearest. (*She gives him a glass of wine.*)

STAUNT. Now run into my room and pour out my drops. But carefully, Helen — take time, take time.

HEL. Yes, father. (*She runs into the bed-chamber*, R.)

STAUNT. Saved! In her eyes.

MAST. (*to* C.). For her own sake, not yours, I lied.

STAUNT. I know it, I know it. You would spurn my thanks. I offer none. I ask for no mercy.

MAST. How came it she did not recognize her own mother's writing?

STAUNT. Her mother's? — Ah, that pain! Her mother's — More wine, Masters. (MASTERS *gives him wine*.) Then you still fancy — Go call Priscilla. I'll tell you all. All — ah! that pain! I must rest first — a short respite — then come — you and Priscilla, and all shall be explained. As you have shown mercy, Masters, so may God himself be merciful!

(*Enter* HELEN, R.)

HEL. Here are your drops, father. And now come and rest. Lean on me, dearest. Why, how you tremble! (*Helping him to rise.*)

STAUNT. Softly, now. There, there. This sudden weakness. What! your arm too, Masters? Well, well; you may come to it yourself — come to it yourself.

(*Exeunt*, R., STAUNTON, HELEN, *and* MASTERS.   *A knock. Enter* MASTERS *again from bed-chamber*, R.)

MAST.   Come in.

(*Enter* AUNT LIBBY, HAL, *and* MAID *with basket*, D. L. *in* F.)

AUNT L.   No. don't set the basket down, Lizzie.   That's for the next place — Well, John, of all persons !   (*Down* C.)

HAL. (L.).   Uncle John, you here !

MAST. (R.).   Hal, why did you never tell me before about these friends of yours ?

HAL.   Why, I tried to this morning, but you were not particularly receptive.

AUNT L.   Where is she, Hal?

HAL.   Oh, ask Uncle John.   He seems to know all about her.

MAST.   If you mean Helen, Hal, she just helped her father into his room.   (*Retires up and seems absorbed in thought.*)

AUNT L.   Oh, then I won't wait.   I only came to find out from Hal where the house was, and to tell her the blanc-mange and some calf's-foot jelly, and a loaf of sponge cake, and a partridge which I shall broil myself, because I never can trust the broiling of a partridge to anybody else, and an air-pillow, which, considering the looks of the room, I doubt if she possesses, together with one or two other little things, would be round at four precisely, and also —

MAID (*up* C.).   Please, ma'am, may I set the basket down ?

AUNT L.   By no means.   I'm going this very moment. John, there's a most interesting case of destitution next door. Six children down with typhoid fever, and their father a good-for-nothing.   I declare, if I hadn't you to look after, and Hal, I'd devote my whole time to charity and — but you are not paying the least attention.   No, don't set the basket down, Lizzie.   Didn't you hear me say I was coming this very minute ?

MAID.   Yes, ma'am.

AUNT L.   And so you may tell the young lady you call Helen, Hal, — and what her last name is I really haven't had time to inquire, though in illness last names or Christian names either, for the matter of that, make very little difference — that —

HAL (*taking basket from* MAID).   Here, set that down.

AUNT L. Why, but, my dear Hal, I'm just on the wing, and I told her distinctly not to set it down. There's nothing so bad as giving servants contradictory orders. It always — come, Lizzie — confuses and upsets them even more than unexpected company to dinner; and that you know, Hal, is a habit I have tried in vain to break your uncle of for years, though to be sure it matters less with these literary men in blue glasses, who might be eating shoeleather for all they appreciate the — but what I started to say was — however, never mind now, because those six children down with typhoid — I really have no time for idle conversation, and — good gracious, Lizzie! do be quick. Go on — go first, for I wish to walk behind and pick up what you are sure to spill. Girls are so careless! Go on now. (*Exeunt* AUNT L. *and* MAID, D. L. *in* F.)

HAL (*up* R., *looking out of window*). I wouldn't have believed it of her. And I trudged two miles out into the country to get them for her!

MAST. (L.). What's wrong, Hal?

HAL. Oh, nothing. Merely when you send some one flowers, and she just sticks them out on the window-sill to wilt — but you're not listening. (*Down* R.)

MAST. (*absorbed*). The same sweet face, but how changed!

HAL. Uncle John, she was anything but pleased to see me this morning. It was you she wanted to see, and now I meet you here, and —

MAST. Stop there, you young idiot! Not a word more. Jealous? Distrustful? Do you wish to end where I did?

HAL. I am not distrustful — only —

MAST. It's men's distrust of women that plays the devil with their lives. O Hal! Hal! the best of us are not worthy to unloose the latchet of their shoes. (*To* C.)

HAL. Uncle John! This from you!

MAST. See here, Hal; if when that sweet young thing comes out again, you do not take her to your heart, and swear to love and cherish her all your life — I'll disown you.

HAL. Are you really in earnest, Uncle John?

MAST. There she comes now. Remember! you have your orders. (*Exit* D. *in* F.)

HAL. (*to* L.). What has happened to Uncle John?

(*Enter* HELEN, R.)

HEL.   Oh, Mr. Masters!

HAL.   What have you done to Uncle John?

HEL. (C.).   Oh, I like him so much.   How gentle he is underneath!   At first, I was afraid of him.

HAL.   Who could help being gentle to you?

HEL.   He used to know my mother.

HAL.   Ah! that explains—

HEL.   But he says I'm not like her.

HAL.   Of course you are not.   (*To* C.)   You are not like anybody in the world.

(*Enter* MRS. G., D. *in* F.)

MRS. G.   Oh, sorry to interrupt, but the sheriff is in my sittin'-room drinkin' his sixth cup of tea to keep him patient.

HAL.   What sheriff?

HEL.   Oh, dear!

MRS. G.   Well, you see, these fine people not being inclined to pay the rent of this *rat-hole*, I had to call in—

HAL.   Rent? Sheriff?   How much do you want?   (*Up* C.)

HEL.   Oh, Mr. Masters!

MRS. G.   Oh, well; if you'll see to things—

HAL. (*taking out purse*).   There—if ever—

MRS. G.   No fear of infection in these notes?

HAL.   'Perhaps you had best fumigate them.

MRS. G.   I will this minute.   (*Exit* D. *in* F.)

HEL.   Oh, Mr. Masters!

HAL.   Why didn't you tell me before?   (*Down* C.) Uncle John was right.   He always used to say women were little hypocrites.

HEL.   Indeed—I—

HAL.   Don't tell me you are not a hypocrite, for you have held me off so at arms' length lately that I cannot help hoping you did it because you—cared for me just a little.   Why, you are not crying!   (*Puts his arm about her.*)

HEL.   I tried to hide it.

HAL.   What! that you cared for me?

HEL.   We are beggars, Hal—and I—did not want you to know how poor we were.   I could not take anything from you, and—

HAL.   And now you won't have to take anything from me, because it will be all yours to start with, my darling.

HEL.   Oh, have you suspected long?

HAL.   I suspected I cared for you almost as soon as I saw you.

HEL. And you'll help me get father well, won't you?

HAL. Yes, dear. (*Aside.*) Poor little girl!

HEL. He's worse again. He's taken such a strange fancy that I mustn't talk to your Uncle John.

HAL. How odd!

HEL. And he wants to see you — but that's not odd.

HAL. You didn't like the flowers I sent you?

HEL. What flowers, Hal?

HAL. Those white lilacs there on the window-sill.

HEL. (*running to window*). Oh. what lovely lilacs! Why did you put them out there without water, to wilt?

HAL (*up* R.). I didn't. I left them on the table.

HEL. I do remember now smelling something sweet, but I was so frightened, so disturbed, I didn't realize who had brought them. Father must have put them there. Isn't it strange? he can't endure the scent! But there is nothing I love so well.

HAL. Forgive me, darling.

HEL. What for?

HAL. For distrusting you just a moment. I thought you had flung them away.

HEL. O Hal! when people love each other there ought not to be any room for distrust.

HAL. I never will distrust you again.

HEL. I read something to-day out of an old letter. It was all so sad and strange. I don't understand it. It was what brought your uncle here. I went to him to try and raise some money on an autograph letter.

HAL. Don't think you must explain anything to me. Whatever you do is sure to be right.

HEL. Dearest! But this letter spoke of a ring, and the motto on the ring was "To love is to trust." Let that be ours, Hal.

HAL. "To love is to trust."

HEL. I mustn't wear these lilacs, on father's account; but I'll just break off a tiny spray — No, you do it for me.

HAL. There, sweet. (*He breaks off a sprig, kisses it, and gives it to her.*)

HEL. And lay it in my prayer-book, and on the fly-leaf I will write, "To love is to trust," and the scent of white lilacs will always bring back to me the sweetest hour of my life.

(STAUNTON'S *voice heard within*, R.)

STAUNT. Helen! Helen!

HEL.   Yes, father.
HAL.   Oh. don't be long.
HEL.   O Hal! with father so ill !
HAL.   Forgive me.   I am a selfish brute where your absence is concerned.   (*Exit* HELEN. R)   Now to tell Uncle John.   There he is in the passage.   Uncle John! (*Enter* MASTERS, D. *in* F.)   Wish me joy. Uncle John.
MAST.   Is it all right?   (*Down* C., *taking his hand.*)
HAL.   Most supremely right.
MAST.   How would next week suit you?
HAL.   What for?
MAST.   The wedding.
HAL.   To-day would suit me better, but women, you know —
MAST.   Well, take your own time.   I'll make all my arrangements. what I shall settle on you, before I go.
HAL.   Before you go where ?
MAST.   To the East.   I'm going to travel for a year or two.
HAL.   Why, isn't this awfully sudden ?
HEL. (*calling outside*).   O Hal! will you come in here a moment ?
HAL (*rapturously*).   Just hear her!   Did you hear her say Hal ?
MAST.   I heard her.   (*Exit* HAL. R.)   It's no use.   All these years my love was a smouldering fire.   Now it flames up with twice its old fierceness.   How can I stay on and be thrown with her and keep silent ?   How can I sit in my lonely house and picture her wifely devotion to that dying wretch whose treachery it would be barbarism to reveal since he is her husband, the father of her child !   Dying !   Hush ! I must not let myself think of that !   And if ever she were free. could I ever forget that she had been his wife !   (*Up* C.) I must see her once more before I go.   (*Looking out of door.*) There she is now !   Priscilla !
PRIS. (*coming to door*).   You spoke, John ?
MAST.   I called you to say good-by, Priscilla.   I leave shortly for the East.   We may not meet again.
PRIS.   For the East !   (*Down* C. *together.*)
MAST.   And now that all is so happily arranged —
PRIS.   So happily — arranged.   (*Aside.*)   Great Heavens !
MAST.   She is a sweet girl, Priscilla.
PRIS.   Yes, John.

MAST. But not as sweet a woman as her mother.

PRIS. You remember her mother?

MAST. Remember her!

PRIS. Is she like her mother?

MAST. Not to my eyes.

PRIS. I never — saw — Helen's — mother!

MAST. Never — saw — Helen's — mother!

PRIS. No. Why do you look at me so strangely, John?

MAST. My God, Priscilla! Are you not Helen's mother?

PRIS. I Helen's mother! Are you dreaming?

MAST. But you are Philip's wife?

PRIS. I am no man's wife.

MAST. (*taking out letter*). Then this letter — this letter you wrote me so long ago —

PRIS. (*taking letter*). What! my letter! And Philip accused himself falsely when he declared but now that he had never delivered it!

MAST. He never did deliver it.

PRIS. How did you come by it?

MAST. Through a Heaven-sent mistake!

PRIS. Then I may speak! I may tell you — O John! why did you lose faith in me?

MAST. Priscilla, it was all a horrible piece of treachery. But you are free? Not Philip's wife?

PRIS. I am no man's wife.

MAST. And he lied to me then. and even now, with death in his face, tried to work on my feelings by added perfidy!

PRIS. God forgive him!

MAST. (*taking her hand*). Oh, if I dared hope!

PRIS. What, John?

MAST. If the words of that letter were true as when they were written. Priscilla, I have never loved any woman but you.

PRIS. John, the words of that letter mean as much now as ever they did.

MAST. (*taking her in his arms*). O Priscilla, my love! after all these years!

PRIS. At last! at last!

MAST. There, weep it out on my breast. Mine — my own!

PRIS. Oh, the wonder of it!

MAST.   And as for that unhappy wretch who tried to **part us** —

(HELEN'S *voice within, sobbing.*)

HEL.   Father!   Speak to me!

(HAL *appears at door,* R., *and holds up a warning hand.*)

PRIS. (*pointing to* HAL).   Hush, John; he has gone to his last account!

CURTAIN.